Sleepover Squad

Sleeping Over

P. J. DENTON

Sleepover Squad

Sleeping Over

Illustrated by Julia Denos

SCHOLASTIC INC.
New York Toronto London Auckland Sydney
Mexico City New Delhi Hong Kong Buenos Aires

This book is a work of fiction. Any references to historical events, real people, or real locales are used fictitiously. Other names, characters, places, and incidents are the product of the author's imagination, and any resemblance to actual events or locales or persons, living or dead, is entirely coincidental.

No part of this publication may be reproduced, stored in a retrieval system, or transmitted in any form or by any means, electronic, mechanical, photocopying, recording, or otherwise, without written permission of the publisher. For information regarding permission, write to Aladdin Paperbacks, an imprint of Simon & Schuster Children's Publishing Division, 1230 Avenue of the Americas, New York, NY 10020.

ISBN-13: 978-0-545-13468-2
ISBN-10: 0-545-13468-4

Text copyright © 2007 by Catherine Hapka.
Illustrations copyright © 2007 by Julia Denos. All rights reserved.
Published by Scholastic Inc., 557 Broadway, New York, NY 10012, by arrangement with Aladdin Paperbacks, an imprint of Simon & Schuster Children's Publishing Division. SCHOLASTIC and associated logos are trademarks and/or registered trademarks of Scholastic Inc.

12 11 10 9 8 7 6 5 4 3 2 1   8 9 10 11 12 13/0

Printed in the U.S.A.   40

First Scholastic printing, December 2008

Designed by Karin Paprocki
The text of this book was set in Cochin.

Sleepover Squad

Sleeping Over

* 1 *

The First Day of the
Last Week of School

"Happy first day of the last week of school!" Emily McDougal said as she walked into the kitchen of her family's old farmhouse. The kitchen was warm and steamy. It smelled like scrambled eggs and potting soil.

Emily's father was sitting at the kitchen table drinking tea and correcting tests. He liked to give the high school students he taught lots of tests. He told Emily it kept them on their toes.

"Thanks, Em," he said. His eyes were the same shade of blue as Emily's, and they crinkled at the corners when he smiled. "Want some eggs? I made French toast this morning too."

"Sure." Emily's stomach grumbled hungrily at the thought of her favorite breakfast. Her father usually had time to make French toast only on weekends.

Just then Emily's mother hurried into the kitchen. Mrs. McDougal hurried everywhere she went. That was how she made her organic plant and vegetable business so successful.

"Happy first day of the last week of school, Mommy," Emily said.

"Does that mean it's summer already?" Mrs. McDougal joked. "Oh no, I'm not ready!" She set the tray of cucumber seedlings she was carrying on the counter. Then she wiped her hands on her jeans and pushed back her wavy blond hair, which was sticking out around her face.

Mr. McDougal was busy fixing Emily a plate of eggs and French toast. "Pour yourself a glass of OJ, Em," he said. "Your mom and I want to talk to you about something before your bus gets here."

"Okay." Emily poured herself a glass of juice, then sat down. What did her parents want to talk about? They didn't look angry or disappointed, like they did when she

forgot to put away her clean laundry or scoop out her cat's litter box.

She didn't have long to wait. "The start of a new season seems like a perfect time for this," her mother announced, sitting down across from Emily. "After all, summer is a time of growth. Spring seedlings sprout up into healthy summer plants, baby animals get bigger and stronger as they explore their new world, all of nature blooms and grows and—"

"All right, Felicity," Mr. McDougal interrupted his wife with a smile. He tapped his wristwatch. "Em and I both need to get to school soon, you know."

"All right, all right," Emily's mother said. "Here's what we wanted to talk to you about, Emily. . . ."

Emily was still thinking about her talk with her parents when she got off the school bus outside Oak Tree Elementary.

She headed straight inside. As usual, her three best friends were waiting for her in the hallway outside their homeroom.

"Guess what?" she cried when she saw them.

"What?" Kara Wyatt asked immediately. Red-haired Kara was almost always the first one to speak up. She said it was because she had to be fast to get a word in around her four noisy brothers.

Meanwhile, Jo Sanchez peered at Emily. "Hey, you look weird," she said. "Is something wrong?"

That was just like Jo. She noticed things. And she was never afraid to ask about them.

Before she answered, Emily looked over at Taylor Kent to see whether she was paying attention. You never could be sure with Taylor. She always seemed to be trying to pay attention to four or five things at once.

This time, though, she was looking straight at Emily with curious, greenish gold eyes. "Well?" she said. "What's the big news, Emmers?"

Next Emily looked around to make sure nobody else was close enough to overhear. This kind of news was for the ears of her best friends alone. After all, they were the only ones in school who knew her embarrassing secret.

"You know my night-light?" she asked them in a quiet voice.

Kara, Jo, and Taylor nodded. Even though all four of them were in the second grade, only Emily still slept with a night-light in her bedroom. Her parents always said it was better that way, even though it made Emily feel like a baby.

"Sure. What about it?" Jo asked.

Emily took a deep breath. Then she smiled. "My parents just told me I can try sleeping without it," she announced. "They finally think I'm old enough."

Taylor gasped. "That's awesome!" she cried, grabbing Emily and hugging her. "Congratulations!"

Emily hugged her back. Over Taylor's shoulder she could see some of their classmates looking in their direction. Taylor's voice could be awfully loud. . . .

"Thanks," Emily said. She was glad her friends understood how important this was. "Don't tell anyone, though."

"Of course not," Kara promised. "We would never breathe a word about something like that."

Emily felt relieved. Her friends' assurances made her already great morning seem even better. "By the way, happy first day of the last week of school, you guys."

"Gracias," Jo said. Emily knew that meant "thank you" in Spanish. Jo's whole family spoke Spanish at home sometimes, especially when her grandfather was visiting. "Same to you, Em," Jo added in English.

"Ooh, you're right—it's the last week of school!" Kara said, looking excited. "That means only a few more days until summer, summer, summer!"

Emily waited for Taylor to say something. But Taylor didn't seem to be paying attention anymore. She was staring down the hall with a faraway look on her face. Emily looked in the same direction, but she couldn't see anything except some third-grade boys giggling and snorting as they played keep-away with someone's baseball glove. There was nothing very interesting about that.

Kara noticed Taylor's faraway expression too. "Earth to Taylor!" she joked.

Taylor blinked, then turned to look at them. She ran one hand over her short, curly black hair. "Sorry," she said. "What were you guys saying?"

"It's the first day of the last week of school," Emily reminded her.

"Oh, I know," Taylor exclaimed, clapping her hands. "That reminds me—I haven't even told you guys my big news yet!"

"What big news?" Kara asked.

Just then the bell rang. It was time for everyone to go into homeroom and take their seats.

"Oops," Taylor said. "Guess I'll have to tell you later."

All morning long Taylor refused to spill her secret. "This is too big to tell in a hurry," she kept saying. "Just wait—I'll tell you at lunch."

For a while Emily thought lunchtime would never arrive. She could hardly wait to find out what Taylor wanted to tell them. Knowing Taylor, it had to be something fun!

Finally, the four friends were sitting in the cafeteria. They always sat at the same table—the small one in the corner near the windows overlooking the playground. That way, they could watch as all the other second and third graders headed outside for recess. Or they could eat in a hurry and rush outside themselves if they wanted.

"Are you going to tell us your big secret now, Taylor?" Kara asked the second she sat down. She tossed her lunch bag on the table without even opening it. "I'm dying of curiosity!"

Taylor grinned. "Really? You look like you're still alive to me," she teased.

"Taylor!" Kara cried, her voice rising to a squeak.

Jo rolled her eyes. "She's just trying to drive you crazy," she told Kara, carefully unpacking her usual lunch: a peanut butter sandwich, a bag of carrot sticks, and a chocolate chip cookie. "Come on, Taylor. You said you'd tell us your big news at lunch, and now it's lunch."

"Yes, please tell us!" Emily begged. "Pretty please!"

Taylor kept grinning. For a second Emily was afraid she would decide not to share after all. Taylor could be like that sometimes. She loved practical jokes and teasing almost as much as Kara's brothers did.

But then Taylor rested her elbows on

the table and leaned forward. "Okay," she said. "Here's my big news. My parents said I could have a party this Friday night to celebrate the start of summer vacation."

"Oh! That sounds like fun." Emily smiled. Taylor's parents sometimes let her have parties when it wasn't even her birthday. The last time had been on Valentine's Day, when Mr. and Mrs. Kent had taken Taylor and her friends to the ice-skating rink. They'd even had heart-shaped pizza for dinner at the snack bar.

"Cool," Kara added. "It's been ages since you had a party, Taylor."

"Oh, but you haven't even heard the best part yet. See, this isn't going to be an ordinary party." Taylor's eyes sparkled as she looked around at them. "It's a *sleepover* party. And you're all invited!"

❋ 2 ❋

Taylor's Big Idea

"A sleepover party?" Kara cried. "Are you serious?"

"Wow!" Jo whistled. "That really *is* big news!"

Emily nodded slowly as her three friends continued chattering about Taylor's surprise. A sleepover—that wasn't just big news. It was huge news. Nobody in the second grade had ever had a slumber party before. But Emily had heard all about what fun sleepovers could be from her neighbor and babysitter, Courtney, who was fifteen.

"We can stay up late," Kara said eagerly. Her cheeks had gone almost as red as her hair, like they always did when she was excited. That made her freckles stand out even more.

"And we can play games like Truth or Dare and Whisper Down the Lane," Jo added.

Kara dumped her lunch out on the table. Her apple bounced across the table and off the edge onto the floor, but she didn't even notice. "And eat lots of junk food and watch scary movies on TV!" she said.

Taylor laughed, her eyes shining. "I knew you guys would love the idea," she exclaimed. "We're going to have the best time ever!"

Emily smiled along with the others. But secretly, she was worried. On the one hand, her friends were right—a sleepover sounded like lots of fun. On the other hand,

Emily's parents had just decided to let her unplug her night-light. Were they really going to let her sleep away from home?

"A last-day-of-school sleepover sounds great," she said. "But I have an even better idea. Why don't we have a picnic at my house instead? My dad can cook his famous garlic hot dogs on the grill, and we can play tag and stuff to welcome summer."

"Are you kidding?" Kara wrinkled her nose. "Picnics are nice, but what could possibly be more fun than a slumber party?"

Emily shrugged, not knowing what to say to that. Just then Randy Blevins, a boy in their class, came running over holding Kara's apple. "Yo, girls, quit throwing food!" he yelled. Randy liked to yell. He yelled at recess, he yelled on the school bus, and he even yelled out the answers in class.

Kara blinked at him in surprise. "Hey,

how did you get my apple?" she demanded. "Give it here."

She grabbed it back. Randy made a monster face and then ran off with a yell.

"You know the best thing about slumber parties?" Kara said with a frown as she wiped off the apple on her napkin. "No boys allowed!"

"Good thing we're having the party at Taylor's house instead of yours." Jo smiled at Kara. "Otherwise, your brothers would probably try to crash it."

Taylor gasped. "That's a great idea!"

"What?" Kara sounded confused. "Having my stinky brothers crash our sleepover? That sounds like a terrible idea to me."

"No, silly." Taylor rolled her eyes. "The great idea is having the next sleepover at your house. Or Em's. Or Jo's."

"The *next* sleepover?" Jo said.

"Sure!" Taylor tapped her fingers on the

lunch table, looking more excited than ever. "This could be just the beginning. Maybe we could have sleepovers every weekend from now on!"

Kara gasped, dropping her apple again. This time it rolled across the table and bumped into Jo's sandwich. "That's the best idea ever!" she cried, clapping her hands. "Taylor, you're a genius!"

"I know." Taylor grinned. "I can't help it."

Jo looked thoughtful. "We could turn it into a club," she suggested. "Sort of like the bridge club my parents belong to."

"Bridge club?" Kara said. "What do they do—go tour bridges or something?"

Jo giggled. "No, silly," she said. "Bridge is the name of a card game. My parents get together with their friends once a month to play cards and eat dinner."

"Oh." Taylor looked confused now too. "So do you want us to play bridge at our party?"

"I don't know how to play bridge!" Kara complained.

"No, wait!" Jo shook her head. "Listen for a second, okay? I'm trying to tell you. My parents have a bridge club—and we should have a slumber party club!"

"Oh!" Taylor and Kara cried at once.

"A—a slumber party club?" Emily repeated, even more nervous than before.

She was already worried about whether her parents would let her go to *one* sleepover. Now her friends wanted to form a whole club?

"It's perfect!" Taylor cried. "We could be the Sleepover Friends."

"No—the Sleepover Squad." Kara smiled. "That means the same thing, but it sounds better. Right, Em?"

Emily smiled weakly. She got the best grades of any of her friends in English class. "Sure," she said. "That sounds good."

She couldn't believe this was happening. The first day of the last week of school had started out great, but now it seemed to be getting worse and worse. What if she asked her parents if she could go to Taylor's slumber party and they said no? What if her best friends were all in the Sleepover Squad without her? They would all be having fun together every weekend, and she would be all alone, sitting in her dark room without even a night-light to keep her company. . . .

Suddenly, Emily felt tears welling up in her eyes. She did her best to stop them by swallowing hard and staring down at her lunch.

But it was no use. Right there at the table she burst into tears.

❋ 3 ❋

Emily's Problem

Kara gasped. "Em, what's wrong?" she cried.

Jo put her arm around Emily's shoulders. "Why are you crying?"

"Did you bite your tongue or something?" Taylor asked. "I hate when I do that. Sometimes it happens when I try to talk and eat at the same time."

Emily shook her head, still staring down at her lunch. Her tears hadn't even stopped yet, but she was already embarrassed about

starting to cry right there in the cafeteria. She hoped the kids at the other tables hadn't noticed.

"I—I'm okay," she said with a gulp and sniffle. She squeezed her eyes shut until she could feel the tears stop flowing. Then she opened her eyes again and wiped them with her napkin.

She looked up at her friends. They were all staring at her with concern.

"Em, what is it?" Jo spoke up for all of them. "You can tell us."

Emily took a deep breath, wishing she wasn't so quick to cry whenever she felt upset or anxious. She knew that Kara and Jo would never cry over something so silly. And Taylor hardly ever cried at all. She hadn't even cried when she'd sprained her ankle in the middle of her big soccer tournament last year.

"It's stupid," Emily said, so quietly that the others had to lean forward to hear her. "But Taylor's party sounds like so much fun, and I'm not sure I'll be able to go!"

"What?" Kara exclaimed. "You have to go! It'll be no fun without all of us there."

Jo was frowning. "Wait, I think I see the problem," she said to Emily. "It's your parents, right? You think they might not let you go?"

Emily nodded. She was afraid if she said anything, she might start crying again.

"Come on, that's silly, Emmers," Taylor declared. "They've let you come to lots of parties at my house before."

"But not slumber parties," Jo told her.

Kara bit her lip, looking worried. "I get it," she said. "Em's parents are awesome and nice and everything. But they can be a little, um . . ." She paused, glancing over at Jo.

"Old-fashioned," Jo finished for her. "At least about some things."

Emily nodded. "I'm afraid this might be one of those things," she said. "What if they say no?"

"What if they say yes?" Taylor said quickly. "You won't know until you ask them, right?"

"Taylor's right," Jo agreed. "We don't even know if this is going to be a problem yet. You can go home and ask them today, and then we'll know—one way or the other."

Kara clasped her hands together, almost knocking over her juice box. "I hope they say yes!" she exclaimed. "The Sleepover Squad wouldn't be the same without you, Em!"

"Don't think that way," Taylor told Kara. "Like Jo said, they haven't said no yet. So maybe they'll say yes, and everything will be fine."

"I hope so," Emily said. But inside, she wasn't so sure. "I guess all I can do is ask, right?"

"Hi, Emily-Memily," Mr. McDougal said with a smile as Emily climbed into the car. "How was school today?"

"Fine." Emily smiled back, then quickly turned around to pull out her seat belt. She was afraid if she said anything else to her father, she would spill out her news about the sleepover. She didn't want to do that — not yet. It would be better to wait until she could talk to both of her parents together.

She had to bite her lip all the way home to keep from telling. It took only about fifteen minutes to drive from Oak Tree Elementary to the McDougals' green-shuttered old farmhouse on a quiet country lane outside of town. But that day it seemed to take forever. Luckily, Emily's father was in a silly mood. He told jokes and sang along with the radio as he drove. That kept him busy enough not to notice that Emily was being extra quiet.

Finally, they turned in past the McDougal Organic Nursery sign by the mailbox. The car bounced down the long gravel driveway between two rows of tall maple trees. "Last stop! All ashore that's going ashore!" Mr. McDougal sang out.

Emily got out of the car. It was a warm, sunny day, and she could see her mother out in the large vegetable garden at the side of the house. "Let's go talk to Mom for a second," she told her father.

"Are you sure?" Mr. McDougal patted his stomach. "I could use a snack. How about if I make us some cinnamon toast?"

"Um, maybe in a few minutes," Emily said. She was so nervous by now that she knew she couldn't possibly eat anything — not even her father's cinnamon toast. "I really want to talk to you and Mom about something."

"Oh!" Her father looked surprised, but he nodded. "Okay, then. Let's go."

They walked over to where Mrs. McDougal was hard at work weeding a lettuce bed. She looked up at them, squinting even under her wide-brimmed straw hat. Then she brushed the dirt off her knees and stood up.

"Hello, you two," she said. "How was school?"

"Miraculous," Mr. McDougal said. "All my tenth graders passed their pop quiz! But never mind that—it seems Emily has something she wants to say to us."

"Oh?" Mrs. McDougal squinted at Emily. "What is it, sweetheart?"

Emily's mouth felt dry. This was it: She was about to find out whether her last day of school—and maybe the rest of the summer, if not her whole life—would be great or terrible.

"Um, okay," she said, shuffling her feet in the dirt. "See, Taylor had a great idea. You know how she's always having parties, right? And they're always lots of fun, and you always let me go? . . . Well, anyway, she had a new idea for a party. It's to celebrate the last day of school. And her parents said it was okay for her to have a sleepover instead of a regular party this time. It would be just the four of us—me, Taylor, Jo, and Kara. We would stay at

Taylor's and play games and stuff just like a regular party, only this time we would bring our sleeping bags and stay over. . . ."

She was talking as fast as she could. She didn't want to give her parents a chance to say no before they heard her out. But finally, she ran out of breath and had to stop.

"So that's what I wanted to talk to you about," she finished. "Can I go? Please?"

Her parents glanced at each other. Emily's heart sank as she saw her mother frown slightly and shake her head. Her father was pursing his lips the way he always did when he was worried about something.

"I'm sorry, Emily," Mrs. McDougal said after a moment of silence. "I don't think so. Not until you're a little older."

❋ 4 ❋

It's Not Fair!

Emily could hardly believe her ears. "Why not?" she cried.

Her father sighed. "As your mother said, it's just too soon, Emily," he said. "Maybe in a year or so we can discuss it again."

"But Taylor's party isn't in a year or so," Emily said. "It's this Friday! Don't you realize how important this is? If I don't get to go—"

She couldn't go on. From the way her parents were staring at her, she knew her arguments wouldn't change their minds. It was just too unfair. She burst into tears and took off toward the house.

Flinging open the mudroom door, she raced inside and almost tripped over her cat, Mi-Mo, who was sleeping on the rag rug just inside. Mumbling an apology to the startled cat, she continued through the room, up the creaky wooden back staircase, and down the hall to her room. Slamming the door behind her, she flung herself onto the handmade quilt covering her bed.

She grabbed her favorite doll, Annabelle. "It's not fair," she mumbled into Annabelle's yarn hair. "It's just not fair!"

She had been worried all day that her parents might say no. But she still could hardly believe that they'd really done it. None of her friends' parents treated them like that, acting as if they weren't old enough to do anything. Emily figured she might as well plug her night-light back in and stay a baby forever. After all, that was how her parents would always see her.

She sobbed into Annabelle's hair for a while longer. Then, all cried out, she sat up and looked around. The afternoon sunlight was pouring in through her windows, making splashes of brightness on the colorful hooked rug on her floor. Standing up, she walked over to the window and looked out. She had a good view of the vegetable garden from there. Mrs. McDougal was still out there weeding, while Emily's father pushed a wheelbarrow toward the compost bins at the edge of the woods.

Emily hurried to her bedroom door and opened it a crack. Mi-Mo was standing outside, swishing his tail. When he saw her, he let out an annoyed meow.

"Sorry, Mi-Mo," she whispered. "Come on in."

She let the cat into her room and then tiptoed out into the hallway, making a beeline for the cordless phone on the little table near the top of the front staircase. Grabbing the handset, she scooted back to her room and closed the door again. Normally, she wasn't supposed to use the phone without asking first. But that day she didn't feel like following her parents' rules.

She sat down next to Mi-Mo, who had just jumped up onto her bed. Then she dialed Kara's number. After two rings someone on the other end picked up.

"Who is it?" a loud male voice barked, making Emily jump.

"Um, hello?" she said. "This is Emily. Is Kara home?"

"Kara who?" the voice demanded gruffly. For a second Emily was afraid she'd dialed the wrong number. Then she heard giggles and snorting in the background.

"Eddie? Chip?" she guessed uncertainly. Kara's two older brothers sounded almost alike on the phone.

There was a sudden burst of muffled yelling in the background. For a second there was no other sound. Then Kara's familiar voice came on the line, sounding a little breathless.

"Sorry about that, Em," she said. "My brothers are idiots. But never mind that—what's up? Did you ask them?"

Emily sighed. "I asked them," she said glumly. "They said no. Just like I was afraid of."

"What?" Kara shrieked so loudly that Emily had to move the phone away from her ear. "You're kidding! I can't believe they said no. Are you sure?"

"I'm sure. They think I'm too young for a sleepover."

"How can they say that?" Kara sounded outraged. "You're practically the most mature and responsible person in the whole second grade. Are they crazy?"

Emily sighed again. She could tell that Kara was trying to make her feel better. But instead, she was feeling worse.

"I'd better get off the phone before my parents come inside," Emily said. "Can you call the others and tell them?"

"Sure. And don't worry, Em—we'll figure out something to do about this!"

"Okay." Emily didn't think there was anything her friends could do that would help. But she didn't tell Kara that. "See you in school tomorrow."

She and Kara said good-bye and hung up. Emily returned the phone to its spot in the hall, then closed herself in her room again. She usually loved hanging out in her room. She had picked out the colors herself—pink and yellow—and helped her mother paint the walls. She had her dolls, two shelves full of toy horses, and dozens and dozens of books crammed into the bookcase her father had made out in his workshop. But that day none of it seemed very interesting.

Mi-Mo was sitting with his front legs tucked under his chest, purring loudly. Emily sat down beside him and stroked his glossy fur. Even that didn't make her feel much better.

Half an hour later she heard her mother calling her downstairs to dinner. Emily groaned and pushed herself off the bed.

"Guess I'd better go down, Mi-Mo," she told her cat, feeling grumpy at the thought of facing her parents again. "I wish I didn't have to, though."

She stomped down the steps and into the kitchen. Her father was standing at the stove stirring something, while her mother set the table with the family's cheerful blue and white plates.

"Can you grab the silverware, Em?" Mrs. McDougal said.

Emily frowned. "Do I have a choice?" she muttered under her breath.

Her mother glanced over at her. "What was that, Emily?"

"Never mind." Emily trudged over to the cabinet and grabbed a handful of forks and spoons, letting them clank together as loudly as possible. She tossed a fork and spoon beside each of the three plates on the table, not bothering to straighten them.

She expected her parents to scold her about that. Instead, she saw them exchange a long, serious look.

"All right, people," her father said a moment later. "I think the vegetables are ready. Let's eat!"

Emily ate as quickly as she could. Her stomach felt kind of funny, and she didn't have much of an appetite. But she knew her parents wouldn't let her be excused until she'd eaten something. So she forced down several spoonfuls of peas and carrots and a whole piece of chicken.

"May I be excused?" she asked as soon as she had gulped down the last of her glass of milk. "Please."

Her parents exchanged another glance. Mrs. McDougal's face wore a slight frown, and Mr. McDougal looked somber.

But once again, neither of them said anything about Emily's unusual behavior.

"Yes, you're excused," Mrs. McDougal said.

"Thanks," Emily muttered sullenly. Pushing back her chair, she ran back upstairs.

❊ 5 ❊

Jo's Plan

"O kay," Taylor said. "We need a plan."

The four friends were huddled around Emily's desk in Ms. Byrd's homeroom. As promised, Kara had called the others the previous afternoon to tell them what Emily's parents had said. Emily had filled them all in on the rest of the details when she'd first arrived at school that morning. Now they were all trying to figure out what to do about it.

"What kind of plan?" Emily asked hopelessly. "You guys know my parents. They hardly ever change their minds about stuff."

"Hey, they just agreed to let you turn off your night-light, right?" Kara pointed out. "Maybe they'll see the light about this, too." She grinned. "Get it? See the *light*? Like night-*light*?"

Jo rolled her eyes. "Hardy har har," she said. "Maybe you should do your stand-up comedy routine at the sleepover, Kara."

Emily bit her lip and glanced around the room, which was filling up with her classmates. She was afraid she was about to embarrass herself by starting to cry again.

"Yeah," she said. "And you guys can tell me all about it the next day, since I'll have to miss it."

"Don't worry, Emmers," Taylor said, reaching over to give Emily a hug. "That's definitely not going to happen. If you can't come, the sleepover is off. We'll do a picnic or something instead. But I'm not ready to give up yet!"

"Taylor's right," Kara said as Jo nodded. "It wouldn't be any fun without you."

Emily was glad the others didn't want to have the slumber party without her. But that made her feel even worse about the whole situation. Her parents weren't just ruining things for her—they were ruining them for her best friends, too!

"Okay, so all we need is a good plan, right?" Kara said, tipping her chair back against the desk behind her. "So who has a good idea?"

"Maybe we should all go over and talk to Em's parents," Taylor suggested, rubbing her hands together. "We can just keep telling them all the reasons we need Emmers there until they have no choice but to give in."

"I have a better idea," Kara said. "Emily could go on a hunger strike! You're so skinny already, Em—if you swore you wouldn't eat again until your parents changed their minds, they'd have to give in. Oh! Or how about this—the silent treatment. Don't talk to them until they say you can come to the party."

Emily was pretty sure neither of those things was likely to work. "Maybe I'd be better off running away from home and coming to live with you," she told Kara, only half joking. "Your parents would never notice another kid around the place."

Taylor laughed. "Now you're thinking!"

"I have an idea."

Jo's voice was quiet. But all three of the others stopped talking and turned to listen. Emily realized that Jo hadn't said anything for a few minutes and guessed that she'd been busy thinking. That made her heart jumped with a tiny spark of hope. Jo always came up with the best plans.

"What is it, J?" Taylor asked eagerly. "What's your idea?"

Before Jo could answer, Randy Blevins came racing into the room. He was yelling, as usual. His friend Max Wolfe was yelling too. They skidded across the floor, their

sneakers squeaking. Both of them crashed into Marie Torelli's desk, making her scream. Her backpack fell off the desk, and her papers scattered everywhere.

"Uh-oh!" Max yelled.

Randy hooted with laughter. "Marie made a mess!" he shouted gleefully. "Messy Marie!"

Max and two or three of the other boys in the room started chanting "Messy Marie! Messy Marie!" over and over again. Marie and her best friend, Tammy Tandrich, scowled at the boys and started picking up the papers.

Kara wrinkled her nose as she watched. "Boys," she declared with distaste. "Why do they always have to act so immature?"

"Never mind them." Taylor turned back to stare at Jo. "We have more important things to worry about than stupid boys. Now come on, Jojo—tell us your plan!"

ugged. "Okay, but it's not really
nd of plan you guys were talking
ut," she said. "I was just thinking about
how Emily told us she was in a bad mood
after her parents said no, stomping around
and everything."

"I still can hardly believe that part,"
Kara broke in with a giggle. "Em's never in
a bad mood!"

"I guess I was last night," Emily admitted,
feeling a little bit guilty about the way she'd
acted. "I was just so mad about being
treated like a baby — I couldn't help it."

"But see, that's what I'm trying to say."
Jo turned to gaze at Emily. "I think the
best way to change your parents' minds is
to apologize for acting that way."

"What?" Taylor exclaimed. "Why should
she apologize? They're the ones treating
her like a kindergartner!"

"No kidding!" Kara agreed quickly.
"*They* should apologize to *her*!"

"I know, I know." Jo still sounded calm, even though Taylor and Kara were both scowling at her. "But think about it, you guys. After she apologizes, they'll definitely listen if she explains about the slumber party in a more grown-up way."

Emily shook her head, not really sure what Jo meant. "But why?" she said. "They already said no when I tried that before. That's why I was mad in the first place, remember?"

"Okay, but didn't you say you barely had a chance to discuss it before you started crying?" Jo said.

Emily glanced around, hoping nobody else had heard what Jo had said. Luckily, Randy and Max were roughhousing in the back of the room, and most of the kids in the class were back there watching them.

"You don't have to tell the whole world what a crybaby I am," Emily told Jo with a slight frown. "Anyway, this is probably a waste of time. My parents think I'm still a baby, and nothing will change their minds."

Jo shrugged. "But see, that's just the problem. If you act like a baby, they'll keep treating you like one. But if you act more like a grown-up, maybe they'll notice that you *are* growing up."

"Hey!" Taylor said. "Don't be so mean, Jo. Em's not a baby."

"Yeah." Emily could feel tears welling up, and she swallowed hard to stop them. It was bad enough to know that her parents thought she was a baby. If her best friends started to think the same thing, she wasn't sure she could stand it.

Jo put a hand on Emily's arm. "I'm not trying to be mean, Emily," she said. "But think about it. What's the only way your parents might change their minds about letting you go to the slumber party?"

Emily thought about that. "If they think I really am grown up enough to sleep away from home?"

"Right!" Jo said. "And the best way to show them that is *acting* grown up enough. Get it?"

Taylor and Kara exchanged a glance. They both looked doubtful and a little confused.

But Emily realized that Jo was right. Her parents weren't going to change their minds because of some silly hunger strike or give in to Taylor's arguments no matter how long she talked.

No, Jo's plan was the only one that just might work . . . *if* Emily could pull it off.

❋ 6 ❋

Trying Again

Emily's stomach fluttered nervously as she walked out of school that afternoon with her friends. Could she do it? Was she really grown up enough to make Jo's plan work? Or were her parents right—was she still too young to sleep away from home?

"On the ride home, think about all the stuff we helped you come up with," Jo suggested. "You can sort of practice it in your head. Then talk to both your parents together."

"Okay," Emily said. "Thanks, you guys."

"Are you sure you don't want us to come over and help?" Taylor asked.

Emily shook her head. "I think I need to do this by myself."

Her friends waved good-bye. Jo headed toward her bus, while Taylor and Kara, who both walked to school, headed in the other direction. Emily walked to the area in front of the school where parents could pick up their kids. As always, Mr. Purcell, one of the fourth-grade teachers, was there monitoring the pickups, and Emily waved hello to him.

Normally, Emily's father was already waiting for her when she got out. But today there was no sign of the family's old green and brown station wagon. She sat down on the curb to wait.

A girl from a different second-grade class named Wendy Wing walked over to her.

"Hi, Emily," Wendy said. "Looks like your dad is late, huh?"

"Yeah," Emily said. "Maybe he gave one of his students a detention."

Wendy wrinkled her nose. "Is that when they have to stay after school for being bad? I'm glad we don't have detentions yet. Did you know it might rain tomorrow?"

Emily smiled. Wendy always talked like that. She jumped from one subject to another without even pausing for breath.

"I didn't know that," Emily said.

"I like rain," Wendy said, kicking at the curb. "Hey, Emily, I heard Taylor Kent is having a slumber party. Is that true?"

Emily gulped. "You heard that?"

"Everyone is talking about it," Wendy said. "Guess what? I got an A on my spelling quiz."

"That's nice." Emily wasn't really listening to Wendy anymore. She was too worried about what she had just said. If everyone knew about Taylor's party, everyone would also know if it got canceled. And they would probably find out why, too. Everyone would know that Emily was the baby who wasn't allowed to sleep away from home.

She couldn't let that happen. Right then and there, she decided something: If she couldn't go to the party, she would tell her friends that they should go ahead and have it anyway. Even if they had to do it without her.

That decision made her feel sad . . . but also a little bit more mature. And it reminded her that she'd better follow Jo's advice. On the ride home with her father, she would think hard and plan out exactly what to say. Her friends had already given her lots of ideas, so all she had to do was practice so she wouldn't forget anything. It had to be perfect.

"Excuse me, Wendy," Emily said. "I

think I see my dad's car coming."

She stood up as the station wagon pulled in. But when it stopped by the curb, she got a big surprise. Her father was driving, as usual, but her mother was sitting in the front seat beside him!

Emily gulped. It looked as if she wouldn't have time to plan what to say after all.

She took a deep breath as she walked to the car. All she could do was try her best.

"Hello, Emily," her mother said as Emily slid into the backseat. "How was your day?"

"Fine," Emily replied, feeling nervous. "Um . . . Mommy? Daddy? I want to say something."

"Yes? What is it?" her father asked as he drove the car away from the school.

"I'm sorry about the way I acted yesterday," Emily blurted out. She could feel her face turning almost as red as Kara's, and she was afraid she might start crying again.

But she took a few more deep breaths to hold back her tears. After all, mature almost–third graders didn't cry every time they were nervous or didn't get their way.

"Well, thank you for the apology, Emily." Her mother sounded surprised but pleased.

"That's not all," Emily said. "Um, I have something else I want to say. Will you listen all the way through before you say anything? Please?"

In the front seat her parents exchanged a glance and a nod. "Of course," her father said. "Go ahead. Let's hear it."

"It's about Taylor's sleepover." Emily spoke as calmly and carefully as she could. She wanted to sound just as logical and thoughtful as Jo would in her place. "I know you already said I couldn't go. But I hope you'll think about it again. See, I really think I'm old enough and mature enough to sleep away from home. For one thing, you already decided I was old enough to sleep without my night-light. That means I'm growing up. And I think this party is a good way to show that. I can give you all the details about the party, like that it's at Taylor's house, and it starts at five in the afternoon on Friday. I even already planned out what I would need to bring—my nightgown, my toothbrush, a pillow, and a sleeping bag. Taylor already said we can use her toothpaste and washcloths."

Emily paused for breath. She looked at her parents. Her father's eyes were on the road as he drove. But her mother was looking back at her from the front seat, her face thoughtful.

"Is that all?" Mrs. McDougal asked.

"Not quite," Emily said. "I just want to say that if you say no, I'm not going to act like a brat. I promise. And I don't blame you if you say no just because of how I acted yesterday." She smiled hopefully. "But I hope you'll say yes."

Her mother nodded. Then she and Emily's father shared a long look.

Emily held her breath. She had done everything she could. But would it be enough? Would Jo's plan work?

❋ 7 ❋

The Big Decision

That Friday afternoon, Emily sat on a stool in the farmhouse's kitchen and watched her father pull a pan out of the oven. He was wearing an apron with a picture of an artichoke on it, along with a pair of oven mitts. He closed the oven door with his knee and then turned around to face Emily.

"Ta-da!" he said, sliding the pan onto a trivet on the counter. He grabbed a platter out of the cupboard beside the stove and set

it nearby. Then he turned over the pan and shook it, which made a dozen cupcakes tumble onto the platter. "Looks like the cupcakes came out perfectly!" he announced.

"That's nice. They smell good." Emily sneaked a peek at the clock on the wall over the refrigerator. It was three minutes after five. Were her friends already at

Taylor's house for the slumber party?

Her father looked over just in time to catch what she was doing. "Don't worry," he said with a smile. "You won't be late. That clock is fifteen minutes fast, remember?"

"Oh yeah, I forgot." Emily grinned at him. She still could hardly believe her speech in the car the other day had worked. Her parents had said she could go to the sleepover!

Just then her mother hurried into the kitchen carrying a basket filled with strawberries. "I just picked these," she told Emily, handing her the basket. "I thought you could take them to the party."

"Thanks, Mommy!" Emily said, grabbing a berry and popping it into her mouth. "My friends will love these."

"You're welcome." Her mother smiled at her. "Now, are you sure you packed everything you'll need tonight?"

"I think so." Emily glanced at the suitcase, pillow, and rolled-up sleeping bag stacked neatly beside the back door. "I have my nightgown, my toothbrush, my slippers, a hairbrush, and some clean clothes to wear tomorrow. Oh, and I also brought Annabelle."

Her father chuckled. "I'm sure Annabelle will enjoy the party too."

"I know she will." Emily was so excited that she shivered. "Thanks again for letting me go, you guys."

"You're welcome," her mother said again. "But you should thank yourself, too. Your father and I were very impressed by your mature apology and explanation in the car on Tuesday."

Mr. McDougal nodded, licking some cupcake crumbs off his fingers. "That's what changed our minds," he added. "You really are growing up into a mature young lady, Emily. Sometimes we forget that."

Her mother stepped forward and gave her a hug. "Yes. But no matter how mature you get, you'll still always be my baby."

Emily hugged her back with the arm not holding the strawberries. For once, she didn't mind at all being called a baby.

Meanwhile, her father was packing up the cupcakes into a large tin. "We're always going to make decisions we think are right for you, Emily," he said. "But we're also always going to be willing to listen to what you have to say if you don't agree with those decisions."

"That's right," her mother agreed. "All you have to do is talk to us, sweetheart."

"I know. I'll remember." Emily smiled at them. She had never been happier to be a part of her little family. Her parents might be a bit old-fashioned, but they were also the best parents in the world.

Of course, that didn't mean she wanted to stay there in the kitchen with them any longer than necessary—at least not today. She had a slumber party to go to. And she couldn't wait!

"Here we are," Emily's father announced, pulling to the curb in front of Taylor's house.

The Kents lived in a big stone house in one of the nicest neighborhoods in town. Huge, leafy trees lined both sides of the street. The trees' gnarled roots made bumps in the white paved sidewalks, and their branches cast shade over the neatly tended front yards.

Emily's heart felt like it was beating twice as fast as usual. She went over to Taylor's house all the time. But today was different.

"Thanks for driving me here," she said.

"No problem. If I'd stayed home, your mother would have made me help her transplant eggplants." Her father winked and grinned to show he was joking around.

"Come on, I'll walk you to the door."

Soon they were standing on the Kents' broad front porch. Emily set down her sleeping bag. She barely had to knock before the door flew open.

"You're here!" Taylor cried. "Welcome to the slumber party! Hi, Mr. M."

"Hi yourself, Taylor," Emily's father

said. He held out the tin he was holding. "Emily and I made cupcakes for the party. We thought you girls could have fun decorating them before you eat them."

"Yum!" Taylor took the tin. "Thanks!"

Just then Taylor's mother appeared behind her. Mrs. Kent usually wore business suits for her job as a financial consultant. But today she was dressed in jeans and a T-shirt.

"Hello there, Emily," Mrs. Kent said. "Hi, Arthur."

"How are you doing, Trenyce?" Emily's father replied. "Are you sure you're up to dealing with this gaggle of girls all night?"

Mrs. Kent laughed. "I think we can manage. Come on in!"

Emily's father helped her carry in her things. Then he got ready to leave.

"Have a nice time, Emily-Memily," he said as he bent down to give her a hug.

While he was hugging her, he whispered in her ear, "Just call us if you get too homesick and want us to come get you. Even if it's the middle of the night."

"Okay." Emily was glad to hear him say that. But she was pretty sure she wouldn't need to call. "Bye, Daddy. See you in the morning."

After he left, Taylor and Emily carried Emily's stuff upstairs to Taylor's bedroom. Taylor dropped Emily's sleeping bag on her fluffy cream-colored rug. Taylor's room was bigger and fancier than Emily's. The Kents had hired a professional decorator to pick out the furniture, carpet, and curtains. The decorator had also chosen the cream and gold wallpaper. But now the wallpaper was almost completely covered by Taylor's sports and music posters. The posters made the room feel a lot friendlier.

"Just throw your suitcase anywhere,"

Taylor told Emily. "We'll set up our sleeping area later."

"So when are Kara and Jo coming?" Emily asked. "I was afraid I'd be the last one to get here."

Taylor opened her mouth to answer. But right at that moment the sound of the doorbell rang through the house. Taylor grinned. "Sounds like they're here now."

The two girls ran back downstairs just in time to see the Kents' housekeeper, Gloria, open the front door. Kara and Jo were standing together in the doorway.

"Yay! Now everyone is here!" Taylor said.

"Hi, Gloria," Kara said politely. Then she rushed inside, tossing aside her duffel bag. "We're here!" she cried. "So let the slumber party begin!"

❋ 8 ❋

Kara Takes the Cake

"Okay, first things first," Taylor announced. "Everybody change into their pajamas!"

Emily blinked in surprise. She had just helped Kara and Jo carry their things upstairs.

Jo wrinkled her nose. "But it's only five fifteen in the afternoon," she said.

"No, she's right!" Kara exclaimed, bouncing up and down on the edge of Taylor's bed. "It's a slumber party. We have to wear pj's!"

"How do you know what to do at a slumber party?" Jo asked. "You've never been to one before!"

But Kara was already digging through her duffel bag. Taylor ran over to her dresser and pulled out a set of frog-print pajamas.

Emily grinned at Jo. "I guess we'd better do what they say."

Soon all four of them were dressed in their nightclothes. Taylor was wearing her frog pajamas and a pair of fuzzy, neon green slippers. Emily had put on her favorite nightgown, which had a pretty blue and yellow flower pattern and lace around the collar. Kara was dressed in a flouncy, bright pink nightie with ruffles. And Jo had on a pair of plaid flannel shorts, a baggy T-shirt, and dark blue slippers.

"Okay, *now* this is starting to look like a slumber party," Kara declared. "So what are we going to do first?"

"We could decorate those cupcakes Emmers brought," Taylor said. "Or maybe we should go play in the rec room for a while first."

Jo raised her hand. "I vote for the rec room," she said. "I dare any of you to try to beat me at Ping-Pong."

"Is that a challenge?" Taylor grinned. She loved challenges. "You're on!"

They all ran downstairs. Taylor's father was just coming in the front door, his suit jacket slung over one arm.

"Hi, Dad!" Taylor called, not even slowing down as she raced down the hall toward the basement door.

"Hi, Mr. Kent!" Emily, Jo, and Kara chorused as they followed.

"Hello, girls," Mr. Kent said with a laugh as they ran past him.

For the next hour the four friends played in the basement rec room. There was a Ping-Pong table down there, along with a pool table, a suction dart game, a TV with a video-game console, and lots of books and board games.

Then Mr. and Mrs. Kent called them upstairs for dinner. Normally when the girls came over to Taylor's house, they ate their snacks or lunch in the kitchen. Tonight, however, they got to eat in the dining room. Gloria had gone home for the day, but she'd left a pot of her delicious spaghetti sauce bubbling on the stove. Mrs. Kent served the spaghetti to the girls accompanied by salad and garlic bread.

"Is it time for cupcakes yet?" Kara asked as she finished her second helping of spaghetti. She burped, then giggled. "Oops! Excuse me."

"It's definitely time for cupcakes," Taylor said. "Emily's dad's cupcakes are so good!"

"We can't eat them yet," Jo reminded her. "We need to decorate them first, right?"

Emily nodded. "Dad sent along some frosting and other stuff for us to use." She stood and picked up her plate. "Let's clear the table, and then we can get started."

Mr. Kent came in from the kitchen just in time to hear her. "Never mind that, Miss Emily," he said, taking the plate from her. "My wife and I will clear up tonight. You girls go ahead into the kitchen—she's already setting up your cupcake factory in there."

"Thanks, Dad!" Taylor skipped over and kissed her father on the cheek as he bent to pick up another plate. "You're the coolest!"

Within moments, the four of them were seated at the kitchen table. The cupcakes were in the middle of the table, along with a bowl of white frosting. All around them were dishes containing different ingredients the girls could use to decorate the cupcakes.

"Wow," Jo said, surveying the choices. "I never heard of decorating cupcakes with strawberries before."

"Why not?" Kara popped a strawberry into her mouth. "It'll make them a lot more interesting than the boring old plain cupcakes from the grocery store."

They all got to work. There were a dozen cupcakes, so each girl got to frost and decorate three. Emily made her first one with pink frosting and strawberries. Then for the next one she traded Jo for some of her pale green frosting and decorated the cupcake with mint leaves from her mother's herb garden. For the third one she kept the icing white and covered the top with different-colored mini gumdrops.

"There!" Taylor said, putting one last pineapple slice on top of her third cupcake. "It's perfect."

"Mine, too." Kara picked up one of her cupcakes and stared at it hungrily. "So can I eat it now?"

The other girls laughed. Kara was always hungry.

"Wait!" Jo said as Kara started to peel back the cupcake paper. She jumped out of her seat. "I brought the digital camera I got for my birthday. Let me take a picture of all the cupcakes before we eat them."

"Okay." Taylor set down her cupcake beside the others. "But hurry up—I don't think Kara can wait much longer!"

When Jo returned with her camera, the girls posed with their cupcakes so she could take pictures of them. Then Taylor took more pictures so Jo could be in them too. Finally, when Mrs. Kent came in to see how they were doing, they asked her to take some pictures of all of them.

"Okay, now it's time to do something even more fun than decorating cupcakes," Kara said. "*Eating* them!"

The girls ate until they were stuffed. Each of them finished two cupcakes.

"We can save the others until later," Taylor said. "We'll probably get hungry again, since we're going to stay up all night."

"We are?" Jo looked alarmed.

"Definitely!" Kara said. "That's what you do at sleepovers. You stay awake playing games and telling spooky stories until the break of dawn."

Emily clapped her hands. "That reminds me," she said. "I just read this really spooky story—"

"Wait! Hold that thought, Emmers."

Taylor stood up and grabbed the plate with the leftover cupcakes on it. "Last one upstairs is a rotten egg."

They ran up to her room. "Let's set out our sleeping bags before we start the stories," Kara suggested.

"Already? But it's not even nine o'clock yet," Taylor said. "You're not thinking about going to sleep already, are you?"

"No way," Kara said. "But I might need to wrap my sleeping bag around me if Em's story is too scary."

They all unrolled their sleeping bags, arranging them in a circle in the middle of the floor. Even Taylor had brought in a sleeping bag for herself. "I don't want to be the only one with a bed," she pointed out. "That wouldn't be fair."

Then they settled down for some spooky stories. Emily went first. She read a lot of books, so she knew lots of stories. One of her stories was so scary, it made Kara scream.

Then Kara took a turn. Her stories weren't very spooky. But they were funny. Soon the others were laughing so hard, they couldn't sit up straight.

Emily had no idea how much time was passing as they took turns telling stories and jokes. All she knew was that she was having a wonderful time. She wasn't even homesick!

"Hey," Jo said after a while. "It's almost eleven o'clock." She yawned.

"Quit yawning!" Taylor warned. "We're going to stay up all night, remember? Come on, let's have a cupcake. That will give us energy."

She grabbed her last cupcake. So did Kara and Jo. But Emily just stared at hers and groaned.

"I'm still too full," she said. "I don't think I can eat another one. One of you guys can have it."

But after finishing theirs, the other girls

were too full too—even Kara. Taylor picked up Emily's leftover cupcake and stared at it.

"I have an idea," she said. "The first person to fall asleep gets this cupcake stuck to their forehead."

Kara laughed. "That's a great idea!" she exclaimed. "Now I *know* I won't be the first one to fall asleep."

"Me neither!" Emily and Jo said at the same time.

"Good," Taylor said. "Now come on— who's in the mood for a game of Truth or Dare?"

That woke them all up for a while. But as midnight came and went, all four of them started yawning, even as they talked and goofed around. Emily was sure one of the others would give in and fall asleep first. After all, she was used to staying awake for hours reading by the light of her night-light.

Soon it was past one o'clock in the morning. Then it was almost two. Taylor's greenish gold eyes were drooping. Kara was huddled in her sleeping bag with both hands propping up her head. And Jo could hardly say two words without stopping to yawn.

"What time is it?" Emily asked sleepily as Taylor finished another spooky story. She was so tired, she wasn't even sure what the story had been about.

Jo checked her watch. "It's two twenty-five," she said. Then she yawned.

Emily glanced at the cupcake sitting in the middle of the circle of sleeping bags. Her eyes felt heavy, and her head seemed to be stuffed full of wool. She wasn't sure she could stay awake much longer. She wondered what it would feel like to wake up with a cupcake stuck to her head with sticky frosting.

Just then she heard a sound from the

direction of Kara's sleeping bag. It sounded like . . . a snore!

She looked over. Kara's head had dropped down onto her folded arms. Her eyes were closed. As Emily watched, her mouth opened and another snore came out.

"Hey!" Emily whispered to Jo and Taylor. "Look. Kara's asleep!"

That made Taylor sit up and look more awake. She grinned. "You know what that means," she whispered.

Jo giggled. "It's your house," she whispered to Taylor, shoving the cupcake toward her. "You do it!"

Taylor grabbed the cupcake. Emily wasn't sure whether to feel sorry for Kara or to laugh. As she pictured Kara waking up in the morning with a cupcake on her forehead, she couldn't help giggling.

Taylor crept forward, the cupcake held at the ready. She moved it carefully toward Kara's forehead. . . .

Just then Kara's eyes fluttered open. She rolled over and looked up at Taylor sleepily. Taylor was so surprised that she froze in place, still holding the cupcake.

"Hey, thanks," Kara mumbled. She grabbed the cupcake and stuffed it into her mouth.

Emily and Jo started giggling again. Taylor rolled her eyes. Kara finished the cupcake, then rolled over and closed her eyes again. Almost immediately, she started snoring softly.

Taylor started laughing too. "Oh well," she said. "So much for that plan!"

"Maybe we should all go to sleep now," Jo said groggily. "It's late, we're all tired. And we don't want to end up sick or grouchy tomorrow. Otherwise, our parents might not let us do this again."

"That's true," Emily said.

Even Taylor nodded, though she looked a little disappointed. "I guess you're right, Jojo," she said. "We'll have plenty of chances to stay up late at other parties."

Emily smiled, glad her parents had changed their minds so she didn't have to miss this. She snuggled down into her cozy sleeping bag, fluffing up her favorite pillow. "Long live the Sleepover Squad!" she said.

"Long live the Sleepover Squad!" Taylor and Jo echoed.

Emily wasn't sure if either of them said anything else, because a second later she was sound asleep.

❋ 9 ❋

Long Live the
Sleepover Squad!

The next morning Emily woke up to the delicious smell of pancakes. For a second she thought she was in her bed at home and wondered why her mattress felt harder than usual. Then she remembered where she really was and smiled. She sat up and yawned. She felt a little tired but happy.

"Good morning," Taylor said. She was sitting up too. "I was just going to wake you guys up. It smells like Mom is making breakfast."

Emily stretched her arms over her head. "It smells great," she said. "And hey, Taylor, this whole party was really fun. I'm glad I got to come."

"Me too," Taylor said. "And now that you've proved you can sleep away from home, I'm sure your parents will say yes next time, too."

Emily nodded. Taylor was probably right. "Maybe they'll even let me host one at my house soon!" she said.

Jo moaned and rubbed her eyes. "Is it morning already?" she asked. Her voice sounded croaky like a frog, which made Taylor and Emily laugh.

"Rise and shine, sleepyhead," Taylor said. Then she leaned over and poked Kara, who was still sleeping. "Hey! Rise and shine."

It took a while to wake up Kara. But finally, all four of them were up. While they got dressed, they talked about the party and started making plans for the next one.

"I was just telling Taylor, my parents might let me have one at our house soon," Emily told Kara and Jo.

"That would be great," Jo said. "Your house is so much fun."

Taylor nodded. "We can play soccer or softball in your backyard and climb trees in the woods."

"Yeah. And Em's dad is a great cook!" Kara agreed. "Maybe he'll barbecue some hot dogs for our dinner."

"I can ask him," Emily promised.

They were all dressed by then, so they headed downstairs for breakfast. Just as they were finishing their pancakes, the doorbell rang. It was Emily's parents, who had arrived to pick her up.

"Good morning, sweetheart," her mother said, bending down to kiss her on the forehead. "Did you have a nice time?"

"The best!" Emily exclaimed. "We played all kinds of games and told stories and—Oh! The cupcakes turned out great," she added, turning toward her father. "We took pictures."

"Yes, they were delicious, Mr. M," Kara said.

That reminded Emily of how Kara had woken up just long enough to eat that last cupcake. She glanced over at Taylor and started to giggle. Taylor giggled too. Then Jo joined in.

Kara looked confused. "What?" she demanded. "What's so funny?"

They all took turns explaining. Before long even Kara was laughing. "That sounds like something I'd do," she admitted.

Then Emily picked up her things, which Mr. Kent had fetched from upstairs. "Bye, you guys," she said. "Happy first official day of summer vacation."

"Happy first official day of summer vacation to you too, Emmers," Taylor said. "Thanks for coming to my sleepover."

Kara and Jo added their good-byes. Then Emily thanked Taylor's parents and followed her own parents out the door. Her father put an arm around her shoulders as they walked toward the car.

"Sounds like the party was a success," he said.

"It was." Emily smiled up at him. "But I missed you guys."

She saw her parents exchange a glance. "Really?" her mother asked, sounding a little worried.

"Yes," Emily said. "I definitely missed you. But not *too* much." She laughed. "I can't wait for the next slumber party!"

Slumber Party Project:
Frosting Frenzy

Emily and the others had tons of fun decorating their own cupcakes with unusual toppings. Why not give it a try at your next party?

Start with plain cupcakes (homemade or store-bought, chocolate or vanilla—it doesn't really matter).

Buy or make plain white frosting. You can add food coloring to create different colors (ask an adult to show you how).

Then find anything you can to decorate your cupcakes! You can use normal stuff, like sprinkles or chocolate chips. Or you can go crazy-creative and try some more unusual toppings. Here are a few ideas: fresh berries; mint leaves; dried fruit; mini marshmallows; coconut flakes; walnut chunks; or pieces of candy, like gumdrops or peppermints. Use your imagination! One tip: Stick to the sweet stuff. Cupcakes topped with olives or tuna fish are just gross!

Once your cupcakes are decorated, do as the Sleepover Squad did and savor the moment by taking pictures. Make sure everybody at the party gets to pose with her favorite cupcake. Later on, the photos will remind you not only of your fancy cupcakes, but of the whole sleepover.

Then comes the best part of all: eating your creations! Make sure there are no leftovers . . . or you never know what might happen!